GW00503731

Big Jean's
Dog Obedience School

Certificate of Completion

AWARDED TO: **PIG**   BREED: **PUG**

FOR ACHIEVING GOOD BEHAVIOUR

SUCCESS RATE 100% GUARANTEED!

FAIL

trainer
e 1978

No job
too tough

4 6 0287634 8

For the stars over Woodbury St.

Published in the UK by Scholastic, 2022
1 London Bridge, London, SE1 9BA
Scholastic Ireland, 89E Lagan Road, Dublin Industrial Estate, Glasnevin, Dublin, D11 HP5F

SCHOLASTIC and associated logos are trademarks and/or
registered trademarks of Scholastic Inc.

First published in Australia by Scholastic Australia, 2022

Text and Illustrations © Aaron Blabey, 2022

The right of Aaron Blabey to be identified as the author and illustrator of this work
has been asserted by him under the Copyright, Designs and Patents Act 1988.

ISBN 978 0702 32345 4

A CIP catalogue record for this book is available from the British Library.

All rights reserved.
This book is sold subject to the condition that it shall not, by way of trade or otherwise, be lent, hired
out or otherwise circulated in any form of binding or cover other than that in which it is published. No
part of this publication may be reproduced, stored in a retrieval system, or transmitted in any form or by
any other means (electronic, mechanical, photocopying, recording or otherwise) without prior written
permission of Scholastic Limited.

Printed in China
Paper made from wood grown in sustainable forests and other controlled sources.

1 3 5 7 9 10 8 6 4 2

This is a work of fiction. Names, characters, places, incidents and dialogues are products
of the author's imagination or are used fictitiously. Any resemblance to actual people,
living or dead, events or locales is entirely coincidental.

www.scholastic.co.uk

PIG the Rebel

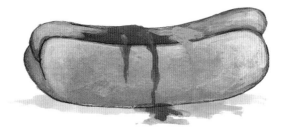

Aaron Blabey

SCHOLASTIC

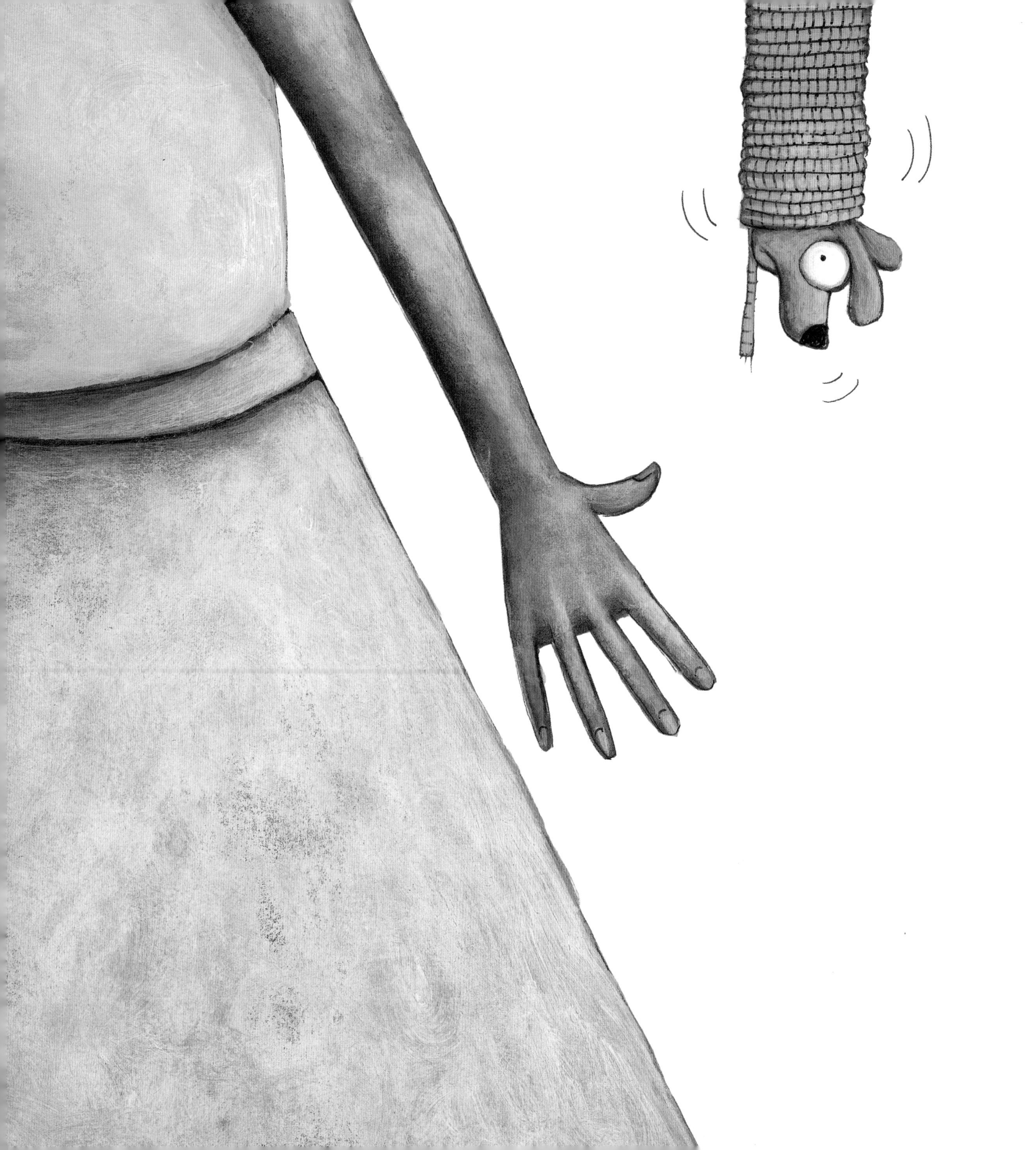

Pig was a pug
and I'm sorry to say,
after years of his antics
it was now time to pay.

Yes, Pig was condemned
to a fate oh so cruel –
it was time for the dreaded . . .

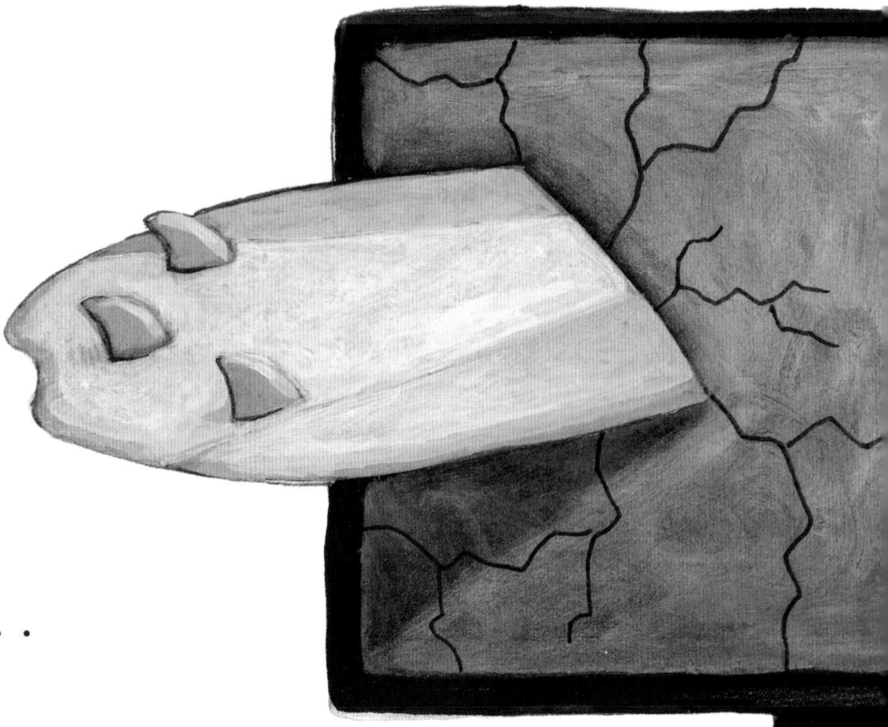

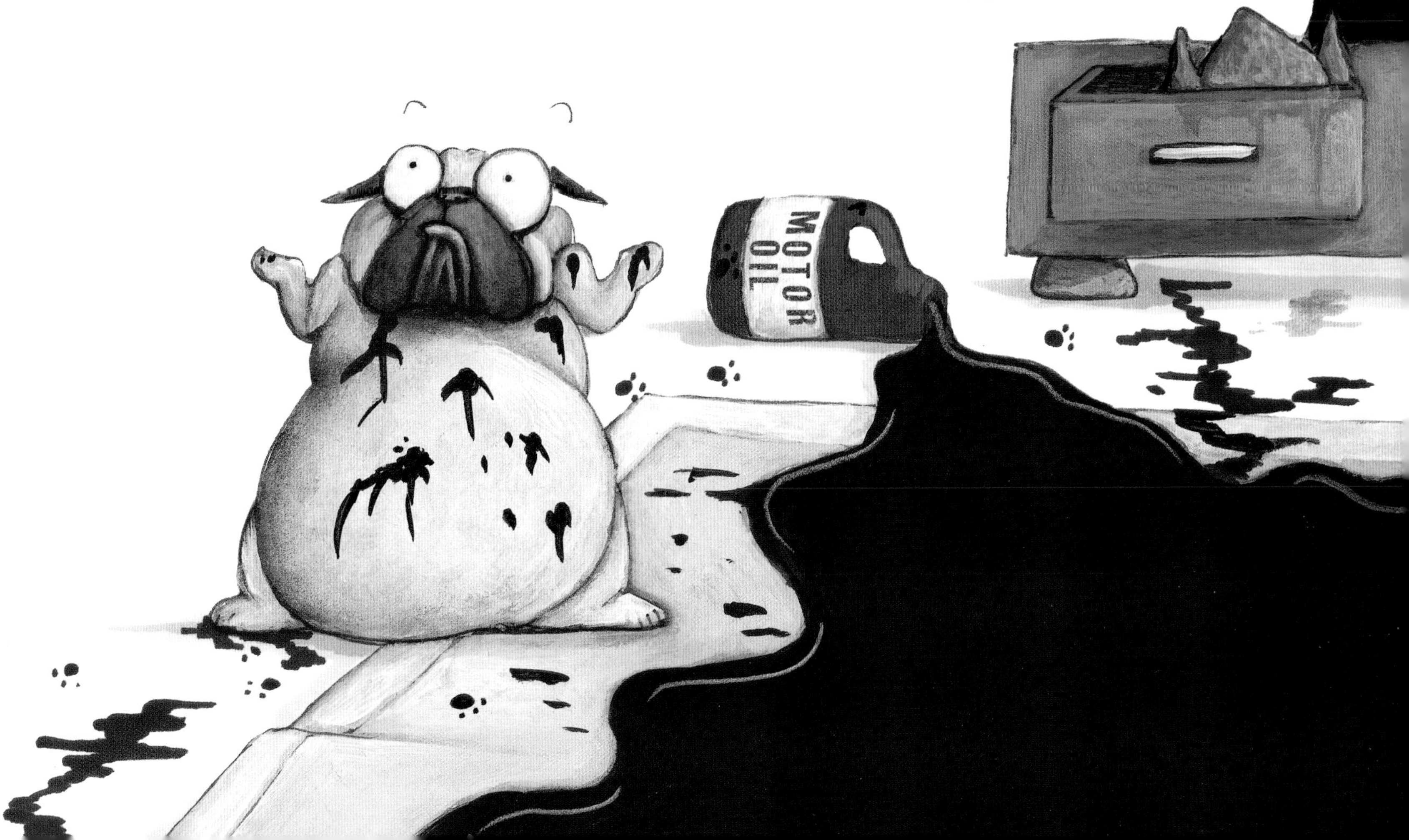
MOTOR OIL

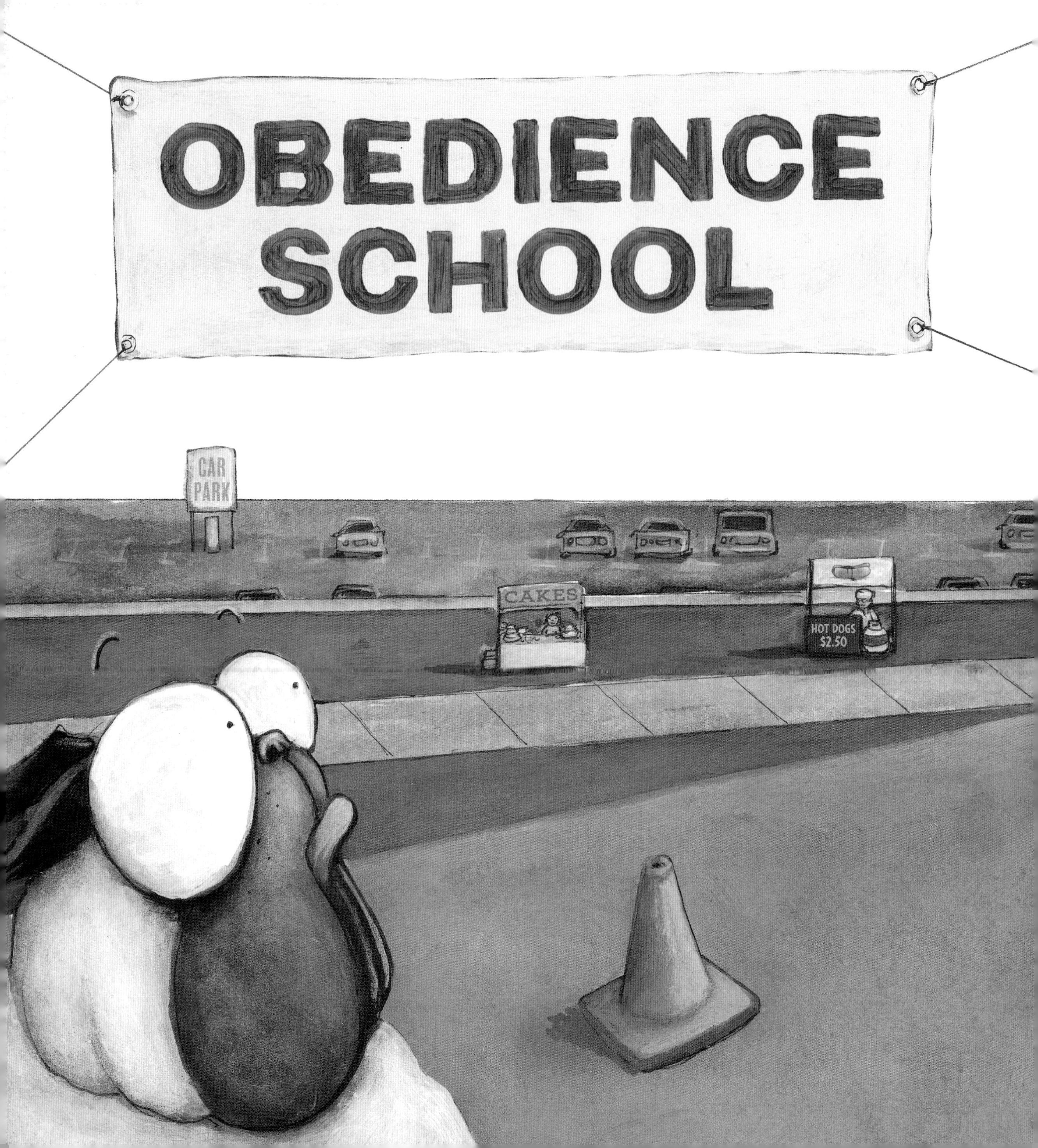
OBEDIENCE
SCHOOL
CAR
PARK
CAKES
HOT DOGS
$2.50

The no-nonsense trainer
looked Pig up and down.
‘I hear you’ve been naughty,’
she said with a frown.

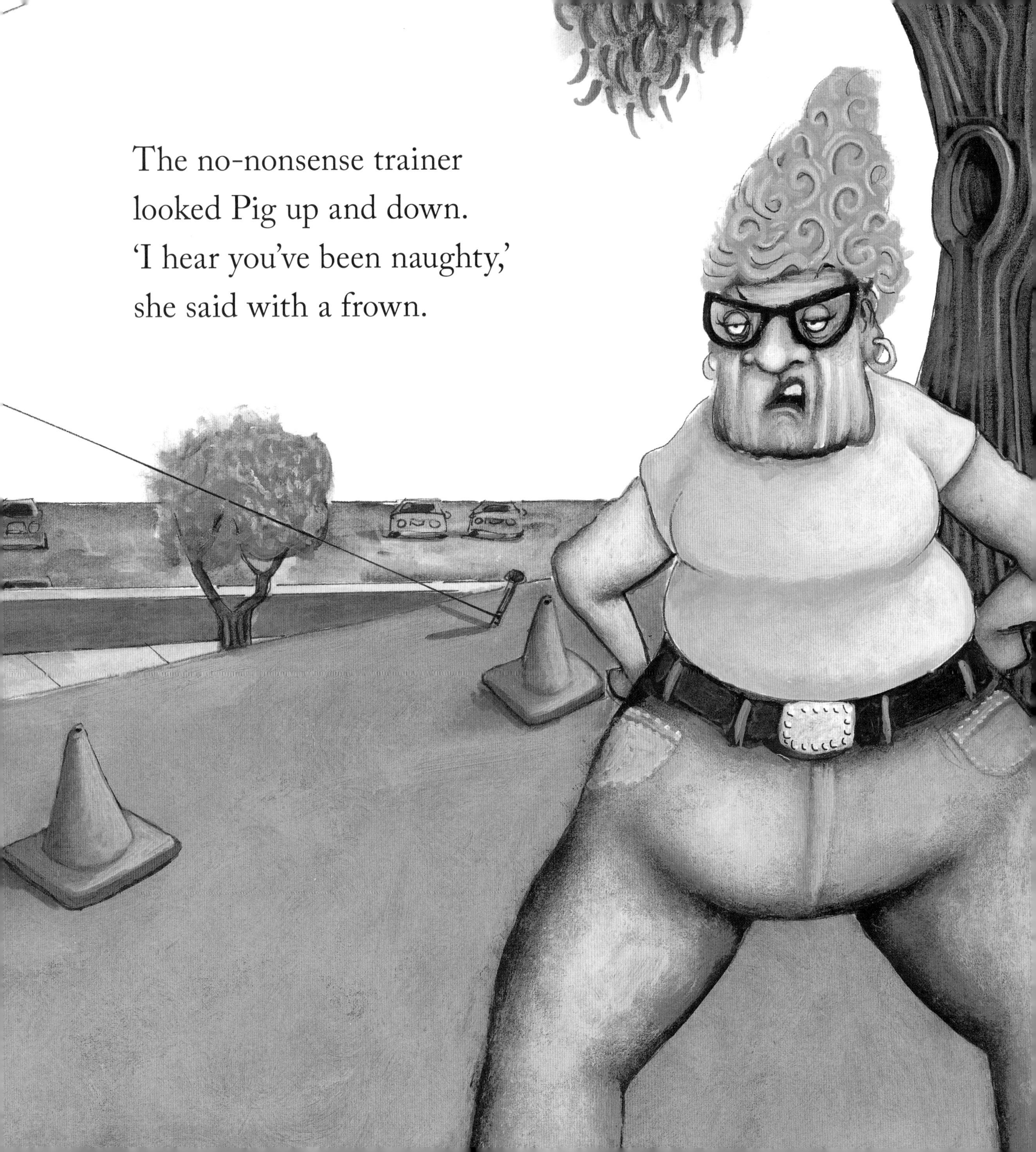

She listed his crimes,
each wretched
endeavour.
Pig pleaded *innocence*,
'What?! Who, *me?*
NEVER!'

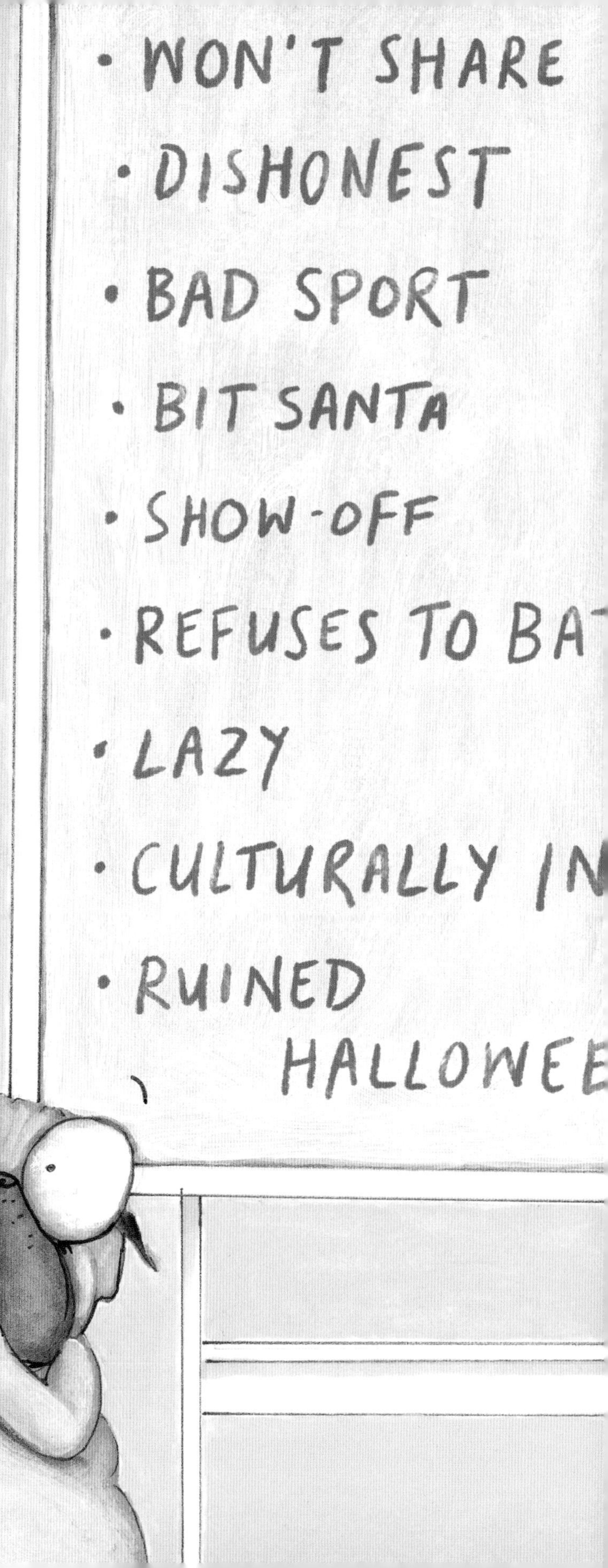

• WON'T SHARE
• DISHONEST
• BAD SPORT
• BIT SANTA
• SHOW-OFF
• REFUSES TO BA
• LAZY
• CULTURALLY IN
• RUINED
HALLOWEE

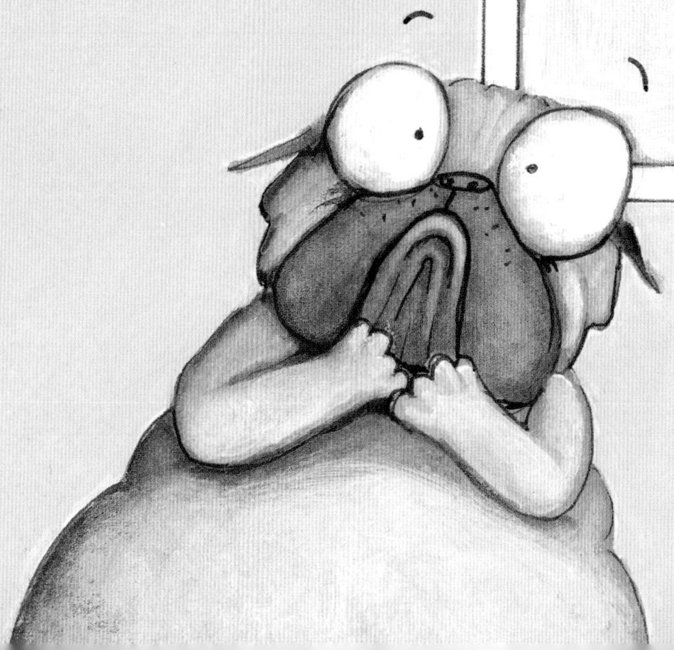

'Hush!' said the trainer.
Her manner was gruff.
'Once you're done *here*,
you'll behave soon enough.'

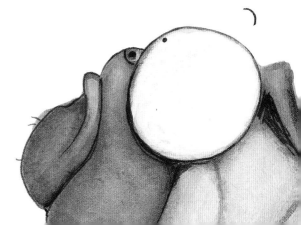

His class was a mixture of various mutts.
They all had their issues.
Some hyper. Some nuts.

A gall’ry of rogues!
A real motley crew!

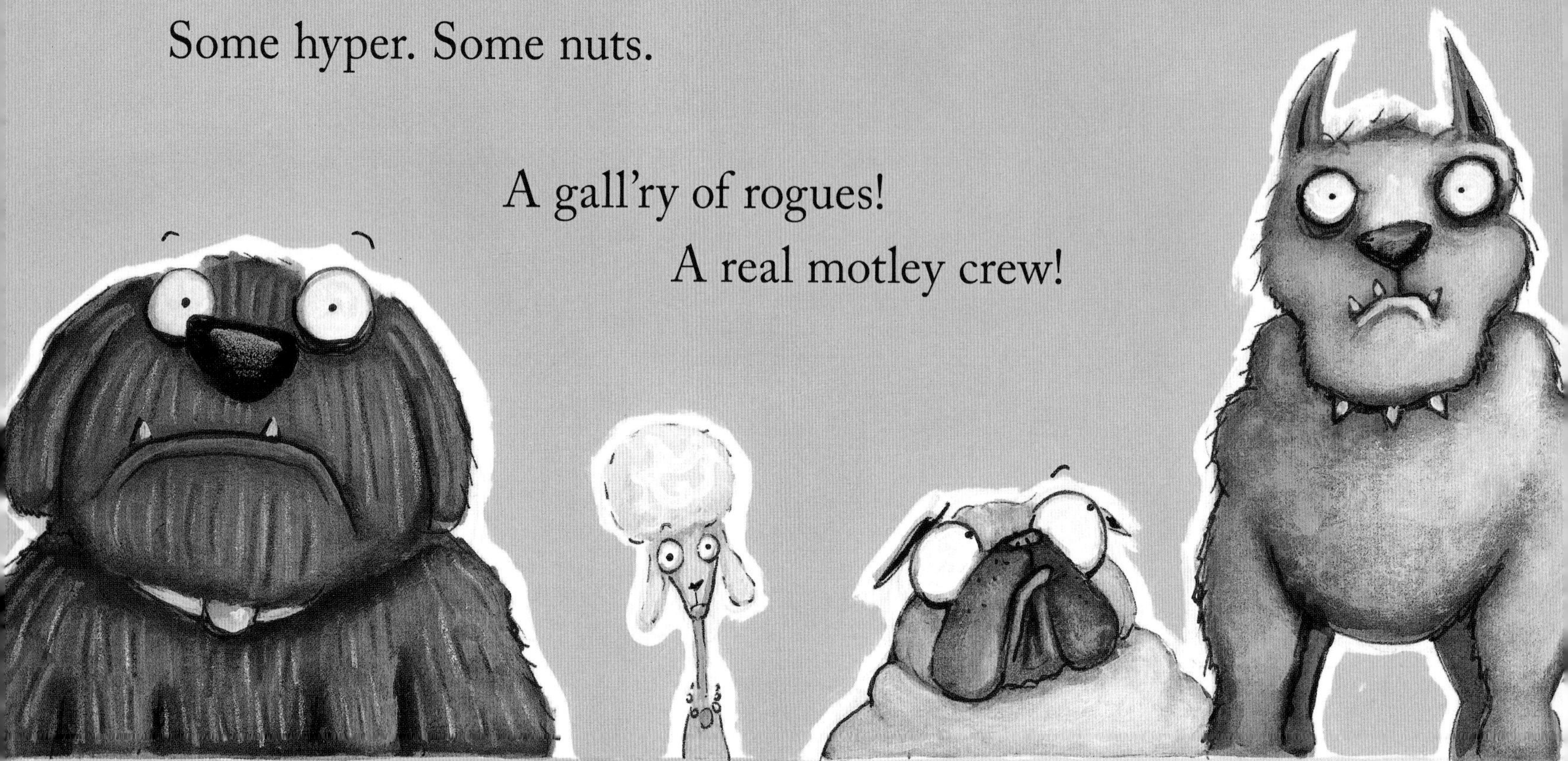

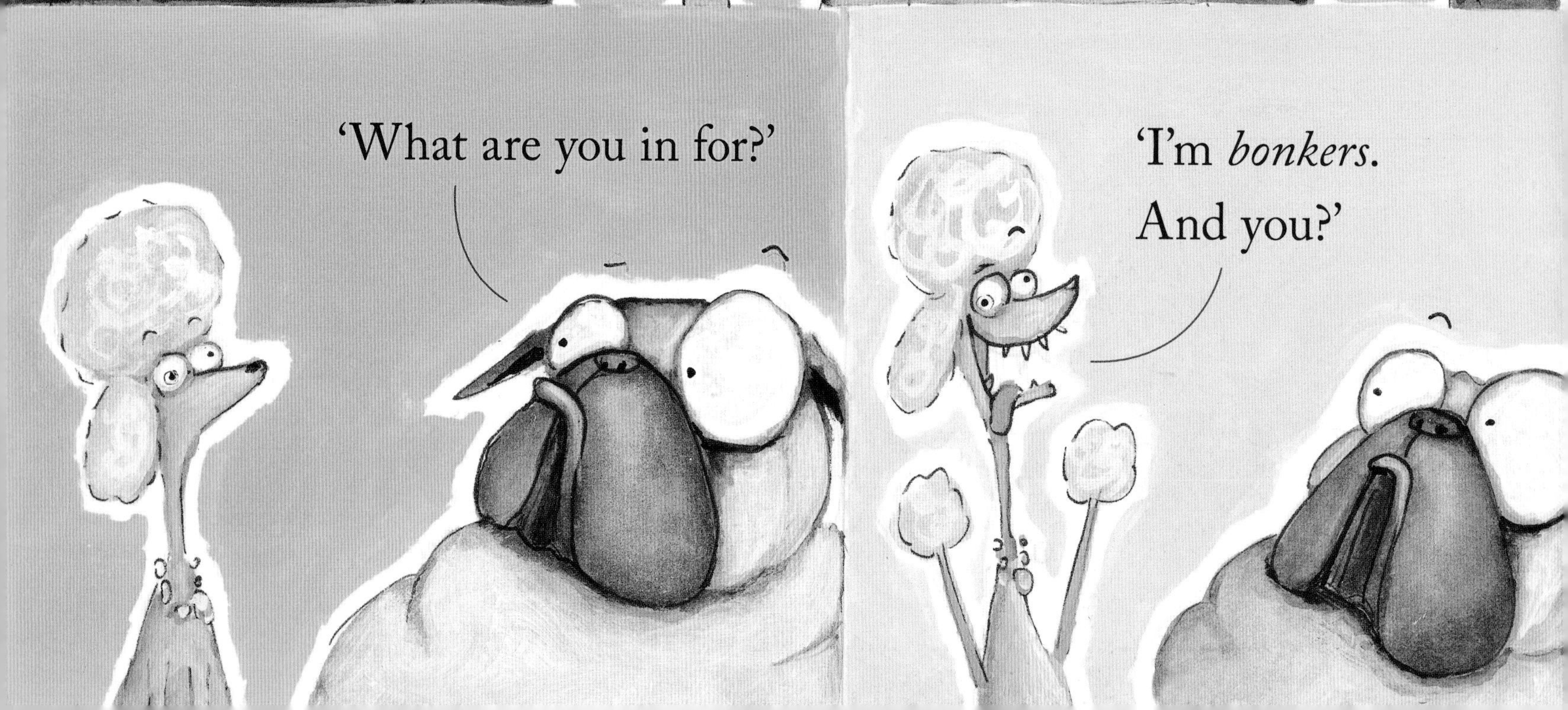
‘What are you in for?’
‘I’m *bonkers*.
And you?’

'CLASS!'
roared the trainer.
'YOU WILL NOW
LEARN TO
SIT!'

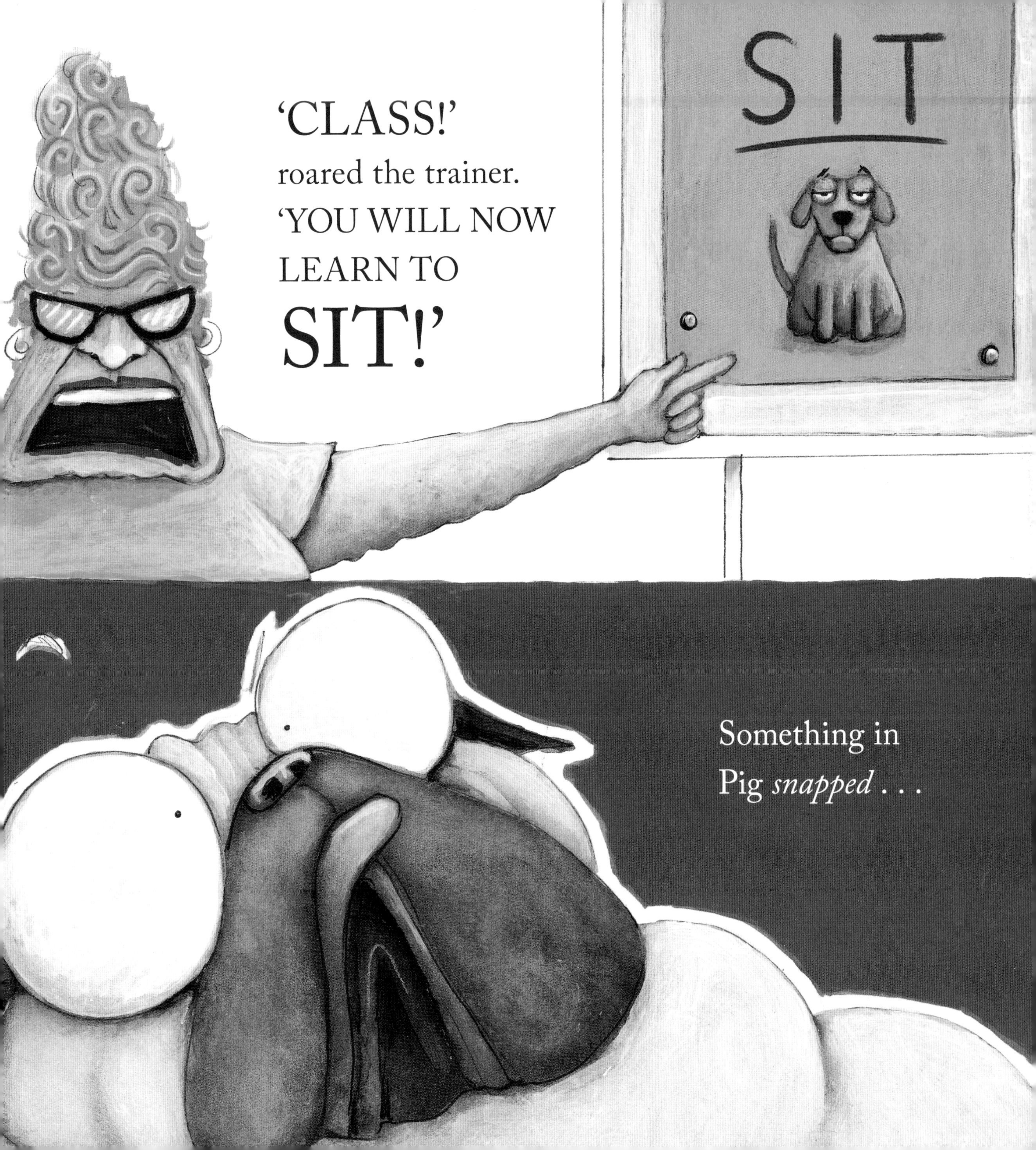
SIT

Something in
Pig *snapped* . . .

He bellowed, *'THAT'S IT!*

NO SCHOOL CAN CONTAIN ME!

LET'S BUST OUT

OF HERE!'

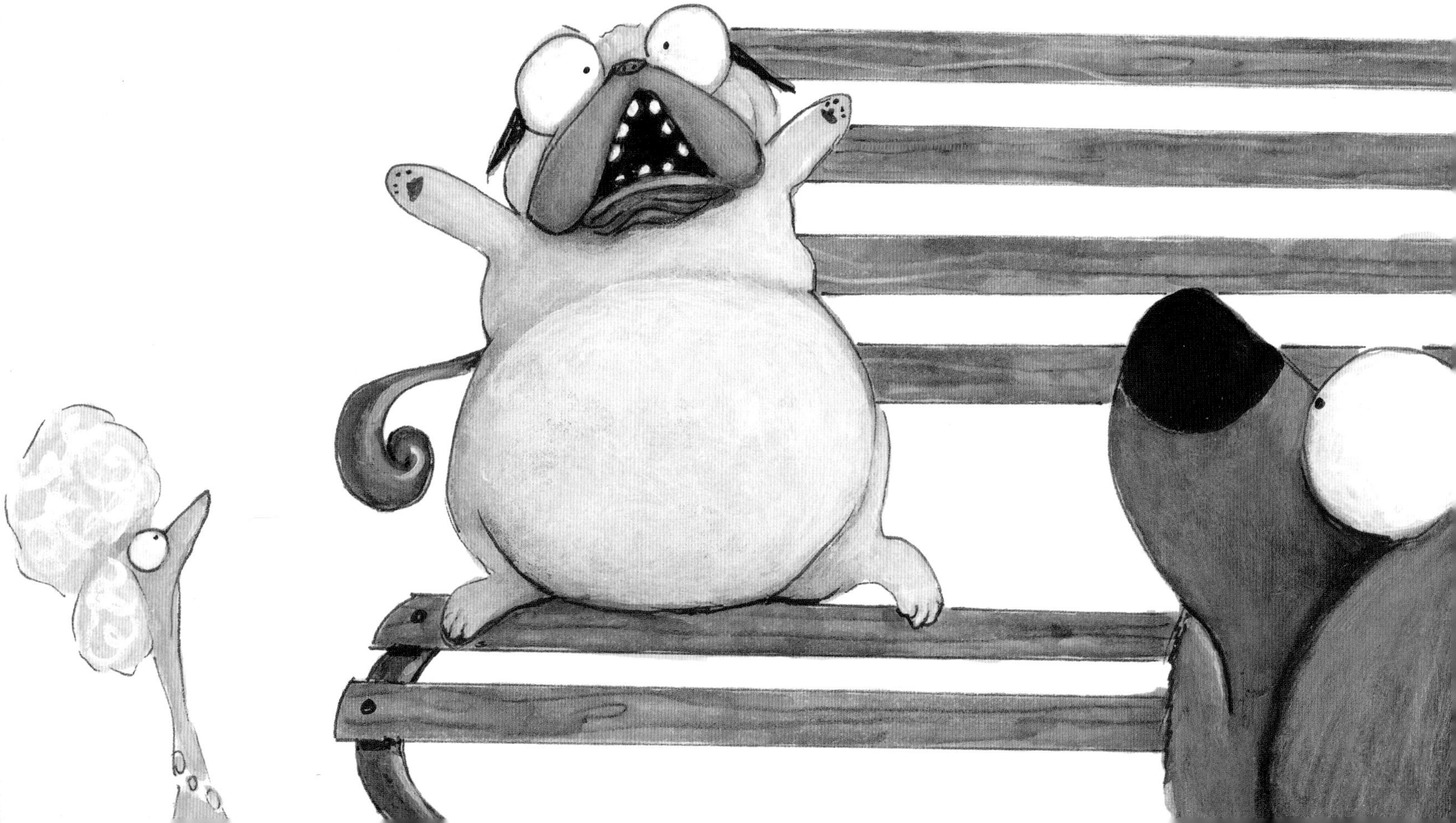

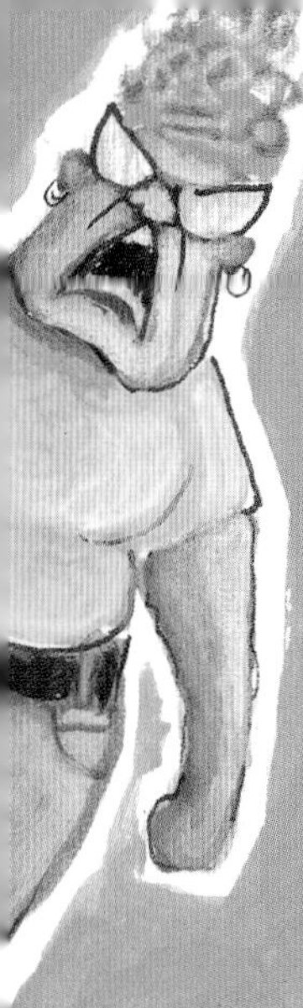

His classmates were stunned,
but they gave a great cheer!

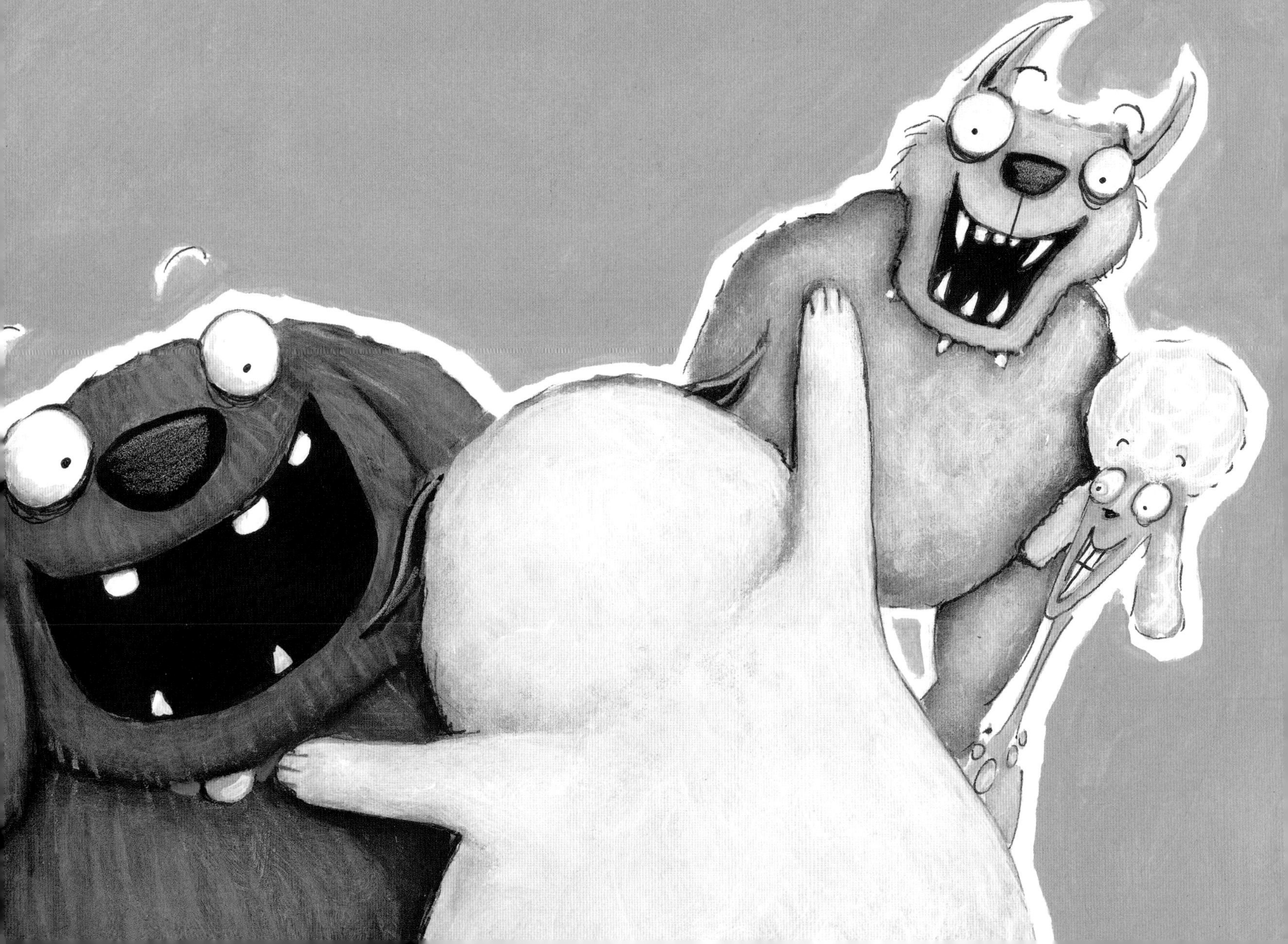

'FOLLOW ME, FRIENDS!'
shouted Pig to his posse.
'LET'S SPLIT FROM THIS JOINT AND THAT TRAINER WHO'S BOSSY!'

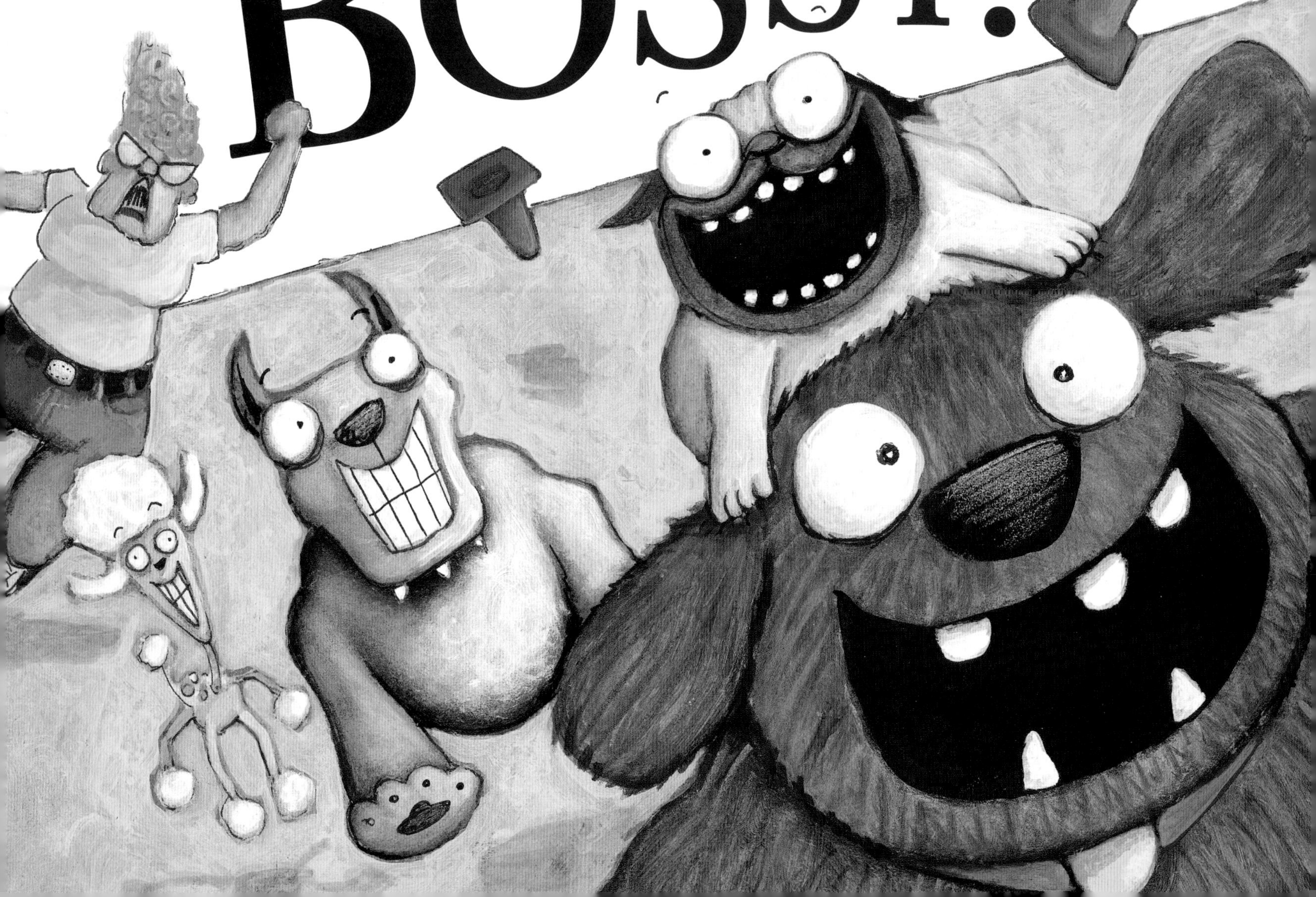

He mounted his steed
and they galloped apace.
But his steed lost its footing . . .

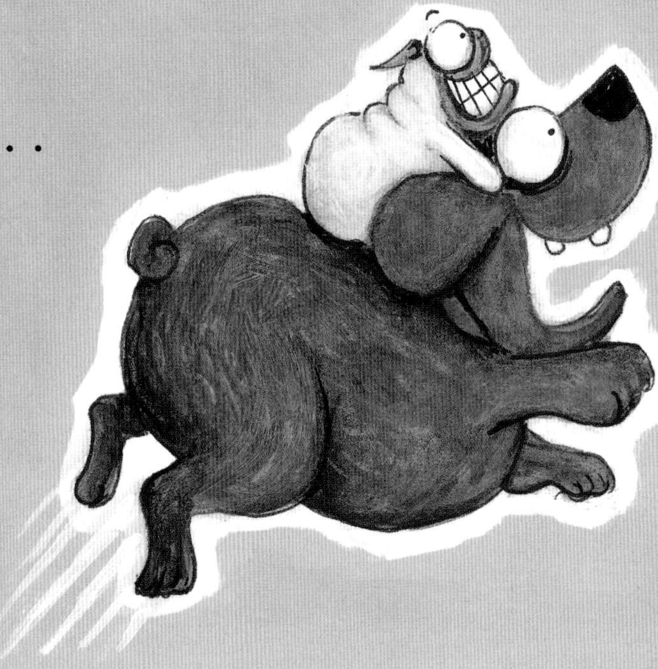

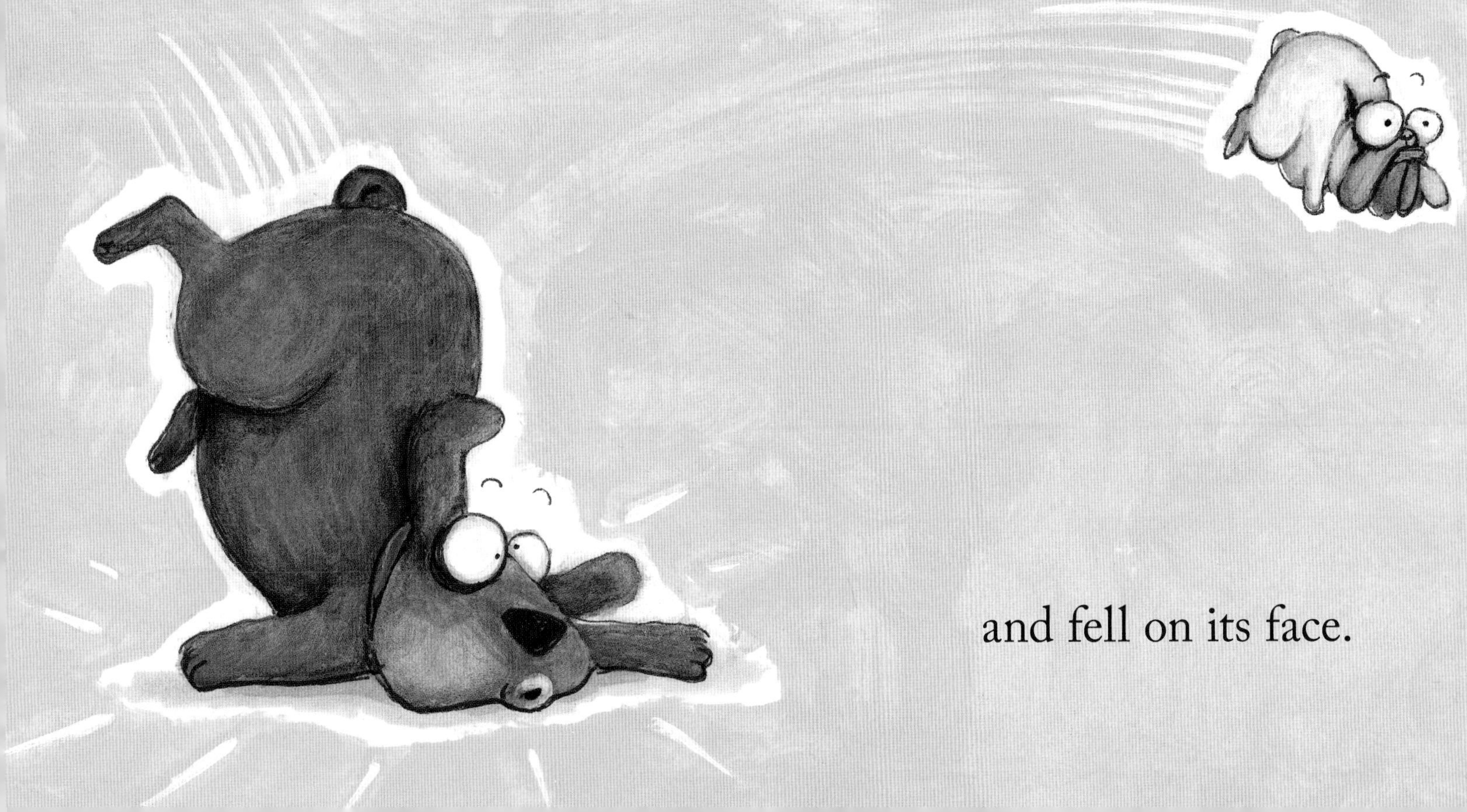

and fell on its face.

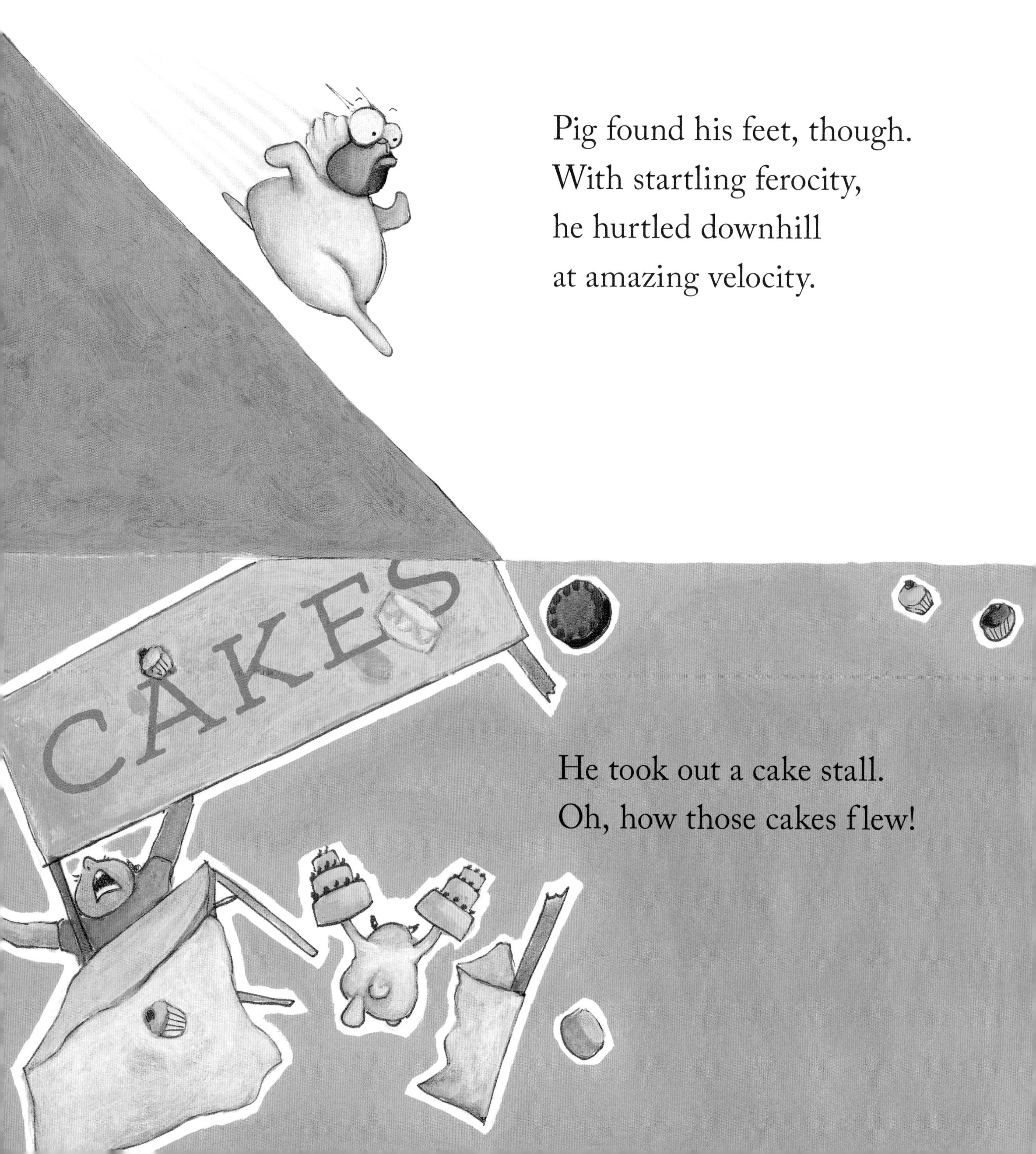
CAKES

Pig found his feet, though.
With startling ferocity,
he hurtled downhill
at amazing velocity.

He took out a cake stall.
Oh, how those cakes flew!

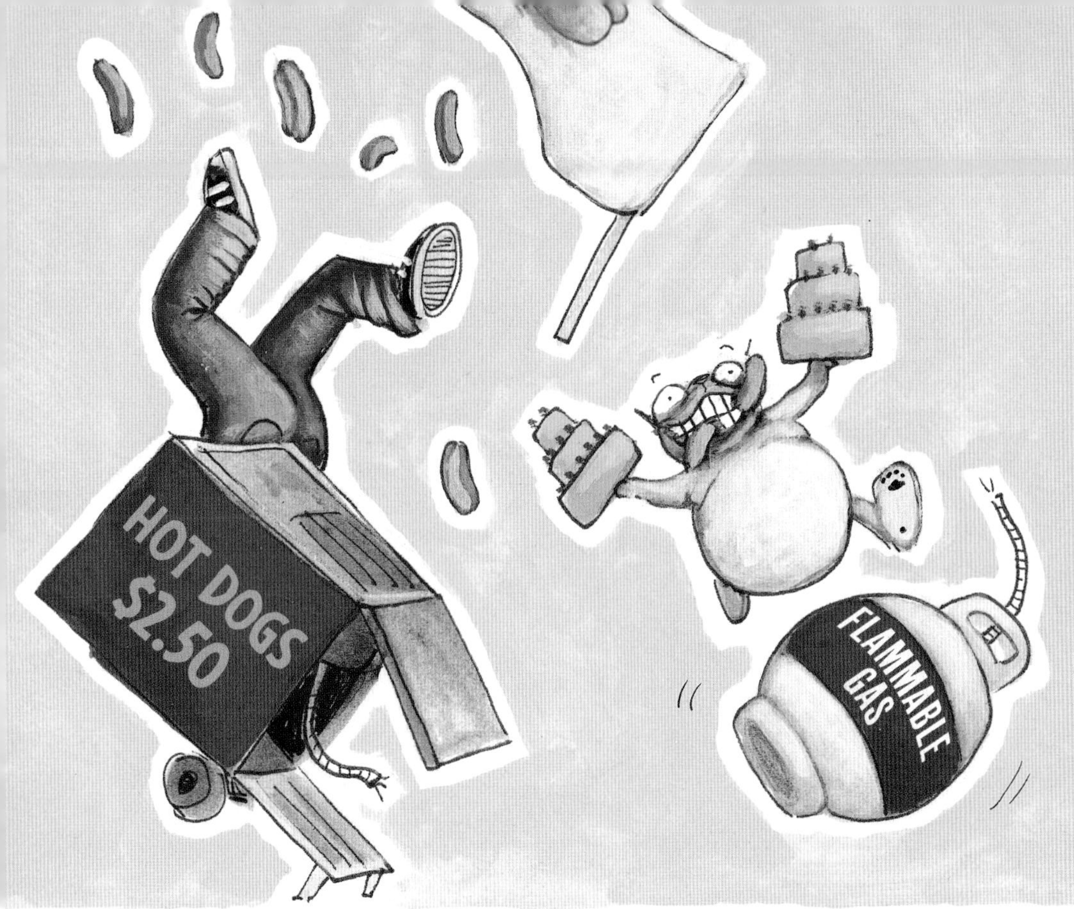
HOT DOGS
$2.50
FLAMMABLE
GAS

He took out the
hot dog guy's
new barbecue . . .

His escape was a triumph!
It really was. Yep!

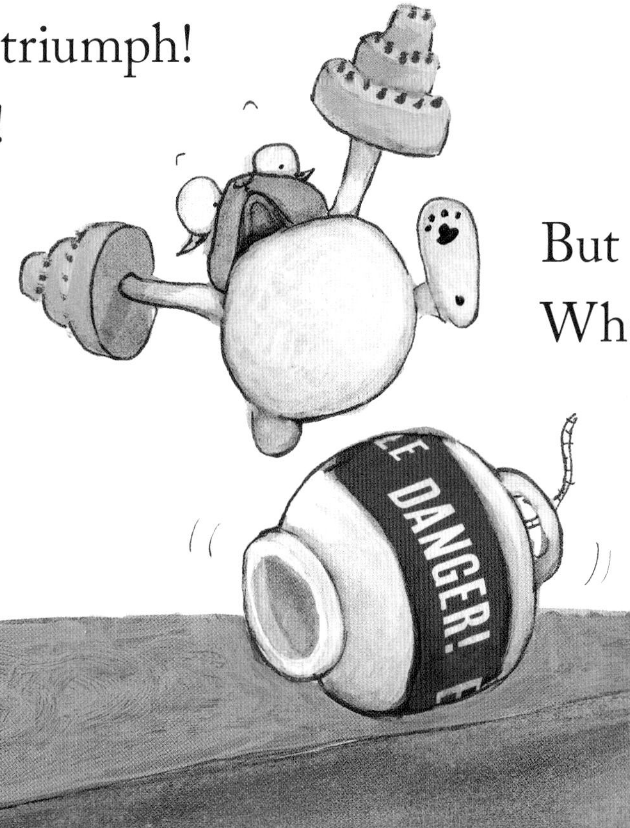
DANGER!

But wait! Hang on!
What's this . . . ?

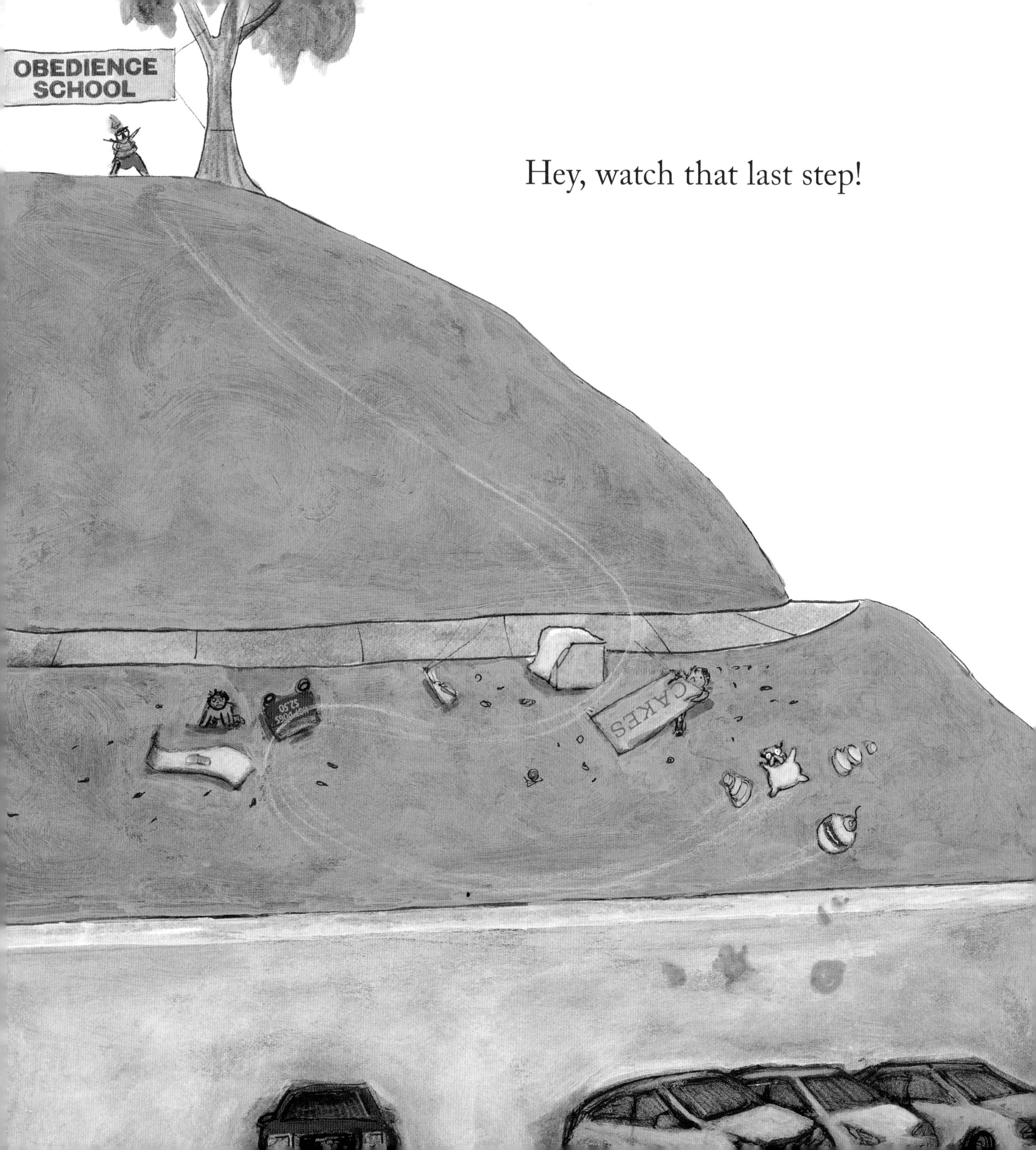
OBEDIENCE
SCHOOL
$2.50
CAKES

Hey, watch that last step!

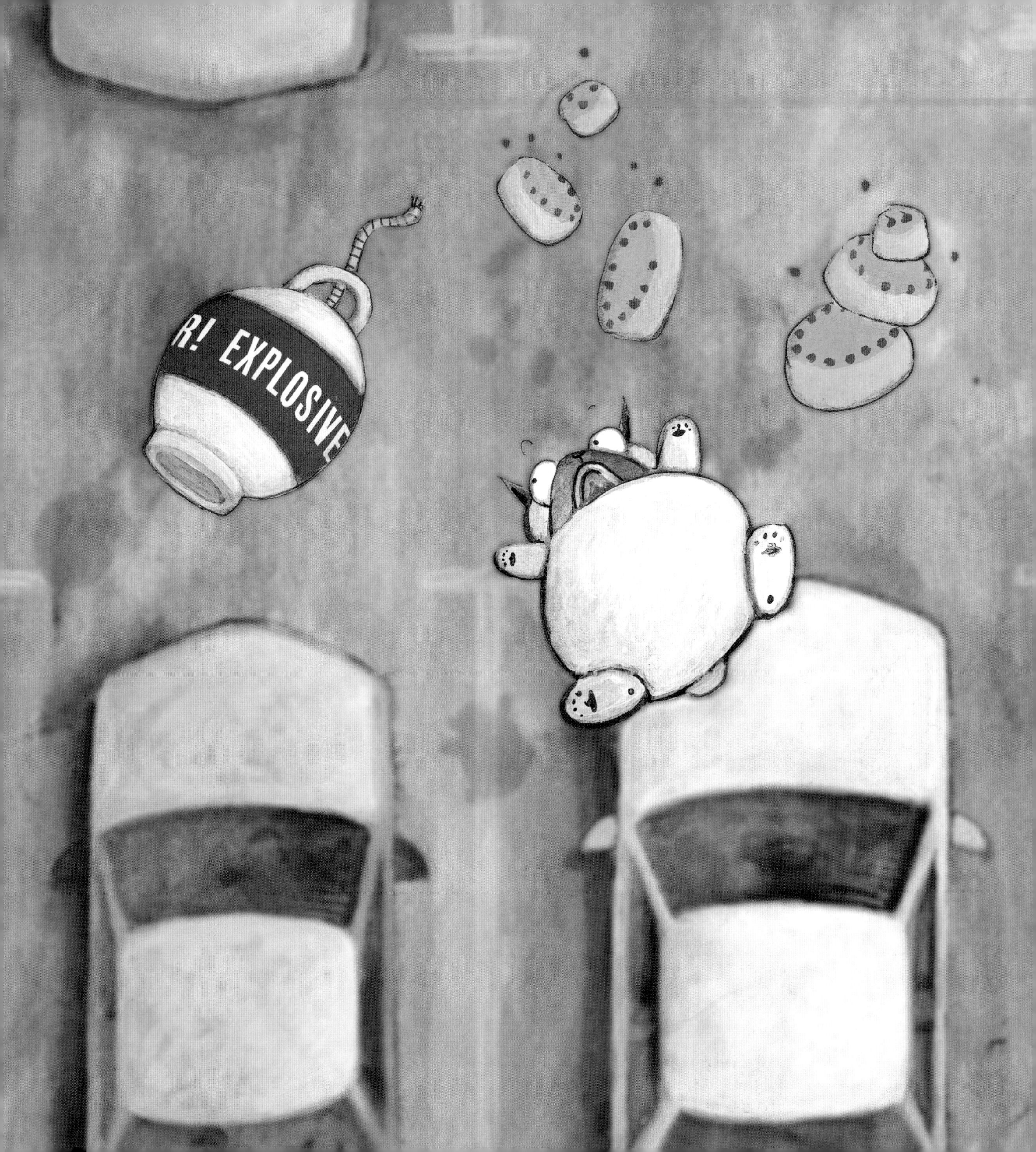
R! EXPLOSIVE

The gas tank went

BOO

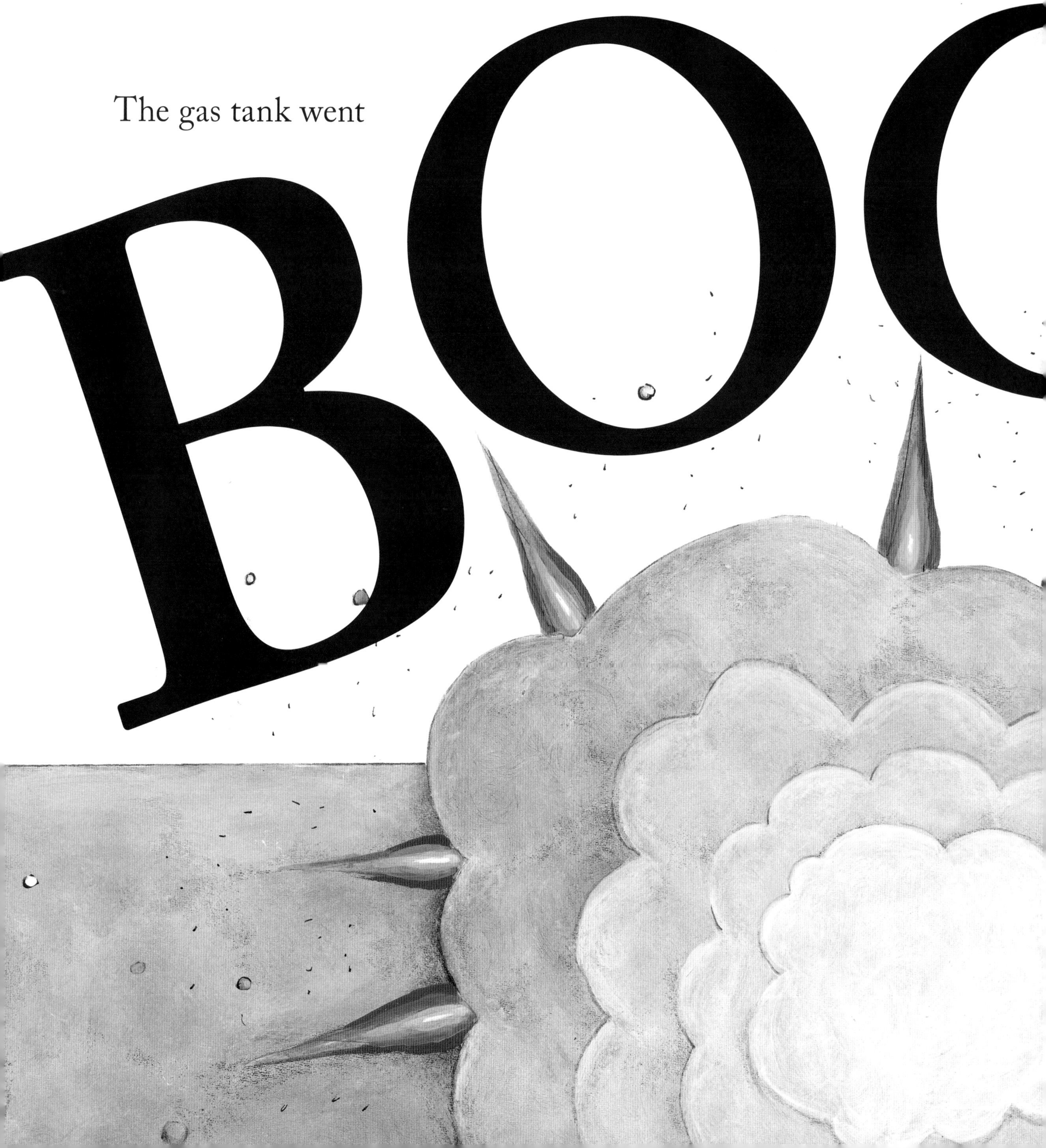

OM!

The sky filled with fur.
It looked like the end.
Oh, it sure did, yes sir.

What happened next?
Oh, how ends the book?
Do you dare turn the page?
Friends, *do you dare look?*

Who could survive
an explosion that BIG?!

Well . . .

. . . one slightly barbecued
pot-bellied PIG.

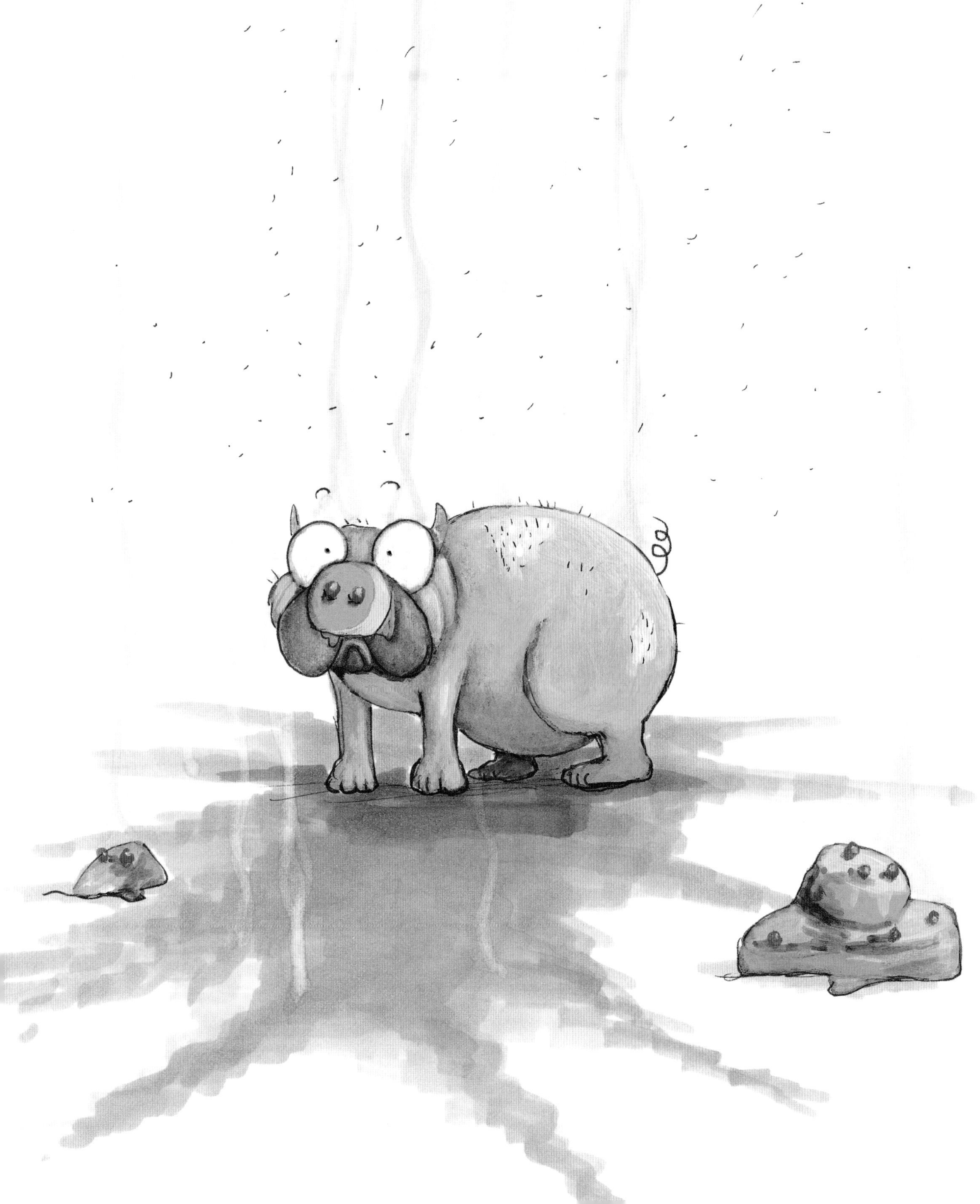

These days it's different,
I'm happy to say.

You've heard this before,
but hey, anyway . . .

His fur all grew back
(he did not need a wig),
and somehow that blast
blew some sense into Pig.

It sparked a new wisdom.
A new way of living –
devoting his future to
sharing and giving.

I know what you're thinking,
'He's fooling you, kid.
He'll NEEEEEEVER change!'

But guess what?

He did.

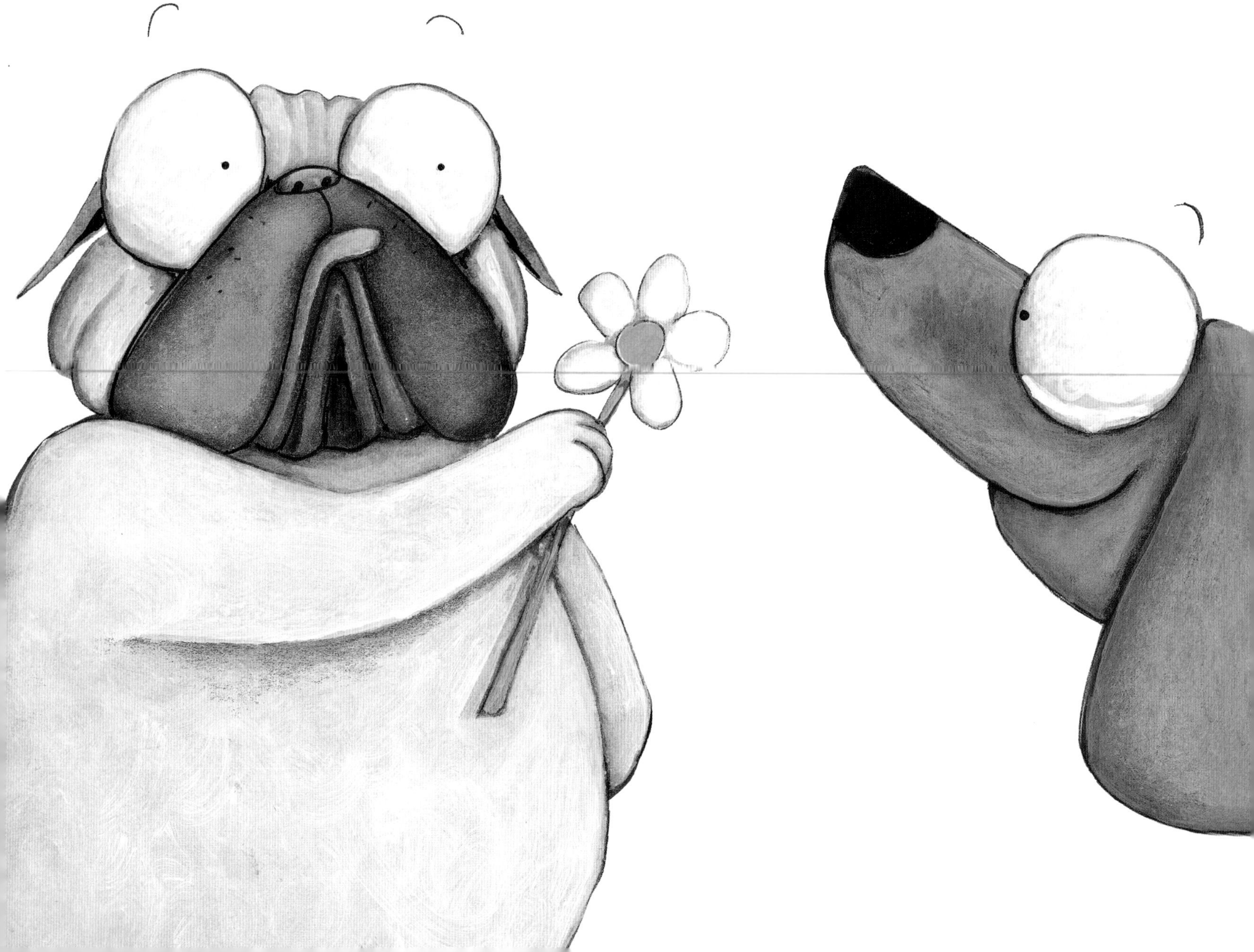

*With love and thanks
to all of you. xo*